Thomas Bailey Aldrich

Pampinea

And Other Poems

Thomas Bailey Aldrich

Pampinea
And Other Poems

ISBN/EAN: 9783744710022

Printed in Europe, USA, Canada, Australia, Japan

Cover: Foto ©Andreas Hilbeck / pixelio.de

More available books at **www.hansebooks.com**

PAMPINEA

AND OTHER POEMS

BY

THOMAS BAILEY ALDRICH

NEW YORK

RUDD & CARLETON 130 GRAND STREET

MDCCCLXI.

CONTENTS.

———•••———

I.

II.

To

MY FRIEND,

BAYARD TAYLOR.

PAMPINEA.

AN IDYL.

———•———

Lying by the summer sea
I had a dream of Italy.

Chalky cliffs and miles of sand,
Mossy reefs and salty caves,
Then the sparkling emerald waves,
Faded; and I seemed to stand,
Myself a languid Florentine,
In the heart of that fair land.
And in a garden cool and green,

Boccaccio's own enchanted place,
I met Pampinea face to face—
A maid so lovely that to see
Her smile is to know Italy!

Her hair was like a coronet
Upon her Grecian forehead set,
Where one gem glistened sunnily
Like Venice, when first seen at sea!
I saw within her violet eyes
The starlight of Italian skies,
And on her brow and breast and hand
The olive of her native land!

And knowing how in other times
Her lips were ripe with Tuscan rhymes
Of love and wine and dance, I spread
My mantle by an almond-tree,
"And here, beneath the rose," I said,
"I'll hear thy Tuscan melody!"

I heard a tale that was not told

In those ten dreamy days of old,

When Heaven, for some divine offence,

Smote Florence with the pestilence;

And in that garden's odorous shade,

The dames of the Decameron,

With each a loyal lover, strayed,

To laugh and sing, at sorest need,

To lie in the lilies in the sun

With glint of plume and golden brede!

And while she whispered in my ear,

The pleasant Arno murmured near,

The dewy, slim chameleons run

Through twenty colors in the sun;

The breezes broke the fountain's glass,

And woke æolian melodies,

And shook from out the scented trees

The bleachèd lemon-blossoms on the grass.

The tale?   I have forgot the tale!—
A Lady all for love forlorn,
A Rose-bud, and a Nightingale
That bruised his bosom on the thorn ;
A pot of rubies buried deep,
A glen, a corpse, a child asleep,
A Monk, that was no monk at all,
In the moonlight by a castle wall.

Now while the sweet-eyed Tuscan wove
The gilded thread of her romance—
Which I have lost by grievous chance—
The one dear woman that I love,
Beside me in our sea-side nook,
Closed a white finger in her book,
Half vexed that she should read, and weep
For Petrarch, to a man asleep !
And scorning me, so tame and cold,
She rose, and wandered down the shore,
Her wine-dark drapery, fold in fold,

Imprisoned by an ivory hand;

And on a ledge of oölite, half in sand,

She stood, and looked at Appledore.

And waking, I beheld her there

Sea-dreaming in the moted air,

A siren sweet and debonair,

With wristlets woven of scarlet weeds,

And oblong lucent amber beads

Of sea-kelp shining in her hair.

And as I thought of dreams, and how

The something in us never sleeps,

But laughs, or sings, or moans, or weeps,

She turned—and on her breast and brow

I saw the tint that seemed not won

From kisses of New England sun;

I saw on brow and breast and hand

The olive of a sunnier land!

She turned—and, lo! within her eyes

There lay the starlight of Italian skies!

Most dreams are dark, beyond the range
Of reason; oft we cannot tell
If they are born of heaven or hell:
But to my soul it seems not strange
That, lying by the summer sea,
With that dark woman watching me,
I slept and dreamed of Italy!

PYTHAGORAS.

ABOVE the petty passions of the crowd

I stand in frozen marble like a god,

Inviolate, and ancient as the moon.

The thing I am, and not the thing Man is,

Fills these deep sockets. Let him moan and die;

For he is dust that shall be laid again:

I know my own creation was divine.

Strewn on the breezy continents I see

The veinèd shells and burnished scales which
  once

Enwrapped my being—husks that had their use;

I brood on all the shapes I must attain

Before I reach the Perfect, which is God,

And dream my dream, and let the rabble go:
For I am of the mountains and the sea,
The deserts, and the caverns in the earth,
The catacombs and fragments of old worlds.

   I was a spirit on the mountain-tops,
A perfume in the valleys, a simoom
On arid deserts, a nomadic wind
Roaming the universe, a tireless Voice.
I was ere Romulus and Remus were;
I was ere Nineveh and Babylon;
I was, and am, and evermore shall be,
Progressing, never reaching to the end.

   A hundred years I trembled in the grass,
The delicate trefoil that muffled warm
A slope on Ida; for a hundred years
Moved in the purple gyre of those dark flowers
The Grecian women strew upon the dead.
   Under the earth, in fragrant glooms, I dwelt;
Then in the veins and sinews of a pine
On a lone isle, where, from the Cyclades,

A mighty wind, like a leviathan,

Ploughed through the brine, and from those
      solitudes

Sent Silence, frightened. To and fro I swayed,

Drawing the sunshine from the stooping clouds.

Suns came and went, and many a mystic moon,

Orbing and waning, and fierce meteors,

Leaving their lurid ghosts to haunt the night.

I heard loud voices by the sounding shore,

The stormy sea-gods, and from fluted conchs

Wild music, and strange shadows floated by,

Some moaning and some singing. So the years

Clustered about me, till the hand of God

Let down the lightning from a sultry sky,

Splintered the pine and split the iron rock;

And from my odorous prison-house a bird,

I in its bosom, darted: so we fled,

Turning the brittle edge of one high wave,

Island and tree and sea-gods left behind !

    Free as the air, from zone to zone I flew,

Far from the tumult to the quiet gates

Of day-break; and beneath me I beheld

Vineyards, and rivers that like silver threads

Ran through the green and gold of pasture-lands,

And here and there a hamlet, a white rose,

And here and there a city, whose slim spires

And palace-roofs and swollen domes uprose

Like scintillant stalagmites in the sun;

I saw huge navies battling with a storm

By ragged reefs along the desolate coasts,

And lazy merchantmen, that crawled, like flies,

Over the blue enamel of the sea

To India or the icy Labradors.

A century was as a single day.

What is a day to an immortal soul?

A breath, no more.   And yet I hold one hour

Beyond all price—that hour when from the sky

I circled near and nearer to the earth,

Nearer and nearer, till I brushed my wings

Against the pointed chestnuts, where a stream

That foamed and chattered over pebbly shoals,

Fled through the briony, and with a shout

Leaped headlong down a precipice; and there,

Gathering wild-flowers in the cool ravine,

Wandered a woman more divinely shaped

Than any of the creatures of the air,

Or river-goddesses, or restless shades

Of noble matrons marvellous in their time

For beauty and great suffering; and I sung,

I charmed her thought, I gave her dreams, and
      then

Down from the sunny atmosphere I stole

And nestled in her bosom.   There I slept

From moon to moon, while in her eyes a thought

Grew sweet and sweeter, deepening like the
      dawn—

A mystical forewarning!   When the stream,

Breaking through leafless brambles and dead
      leaves,

Piped shriller treble, and from chestnut boughs

The fruit dropped noiseless through the autumn
    night,
I gave a quick, low cry, as infants do:
We weep when we are born, not when we die!
So was it destined; and thus came I here,
To suffer bravely as becomes my state,
One step, one grade, one cycle nearer God.

  And knowing these things, can I stoop to fret,
And lie, and haggle in the market-place,
Give dross for dross, or everything for naught?
No! let me sit above the crowd, and sing,
Waiting with hope for that miraculous change
Which seems like sleep; and though I waiting
    starve,
I cannot kiss the idols that are set
By every gate, in every street and park;
I cannot fawn, I cannot soil my soul:
For I am of the mountains and the sea,
The deserts and the caverns in the earth,
The catacombs and fragments of old worlds.

THE TRAGEDY.

———

THE " *Dame with the Camelias* "—
  I think that was the play;
The house was packed from pit to dome
  With the gallant and the gay,
Who had come to see the Tragedy,
  And while the hours away!

There was the faint Exquisite,
  With gloves and glass sublime;
There was the grave Historian,
  And there the man of Rhyme,
And the surly Critic, front to front,
  To see the play of Crime.

21

And there was heavy Ignorance,
    And Vice in Honiton lace;
Sir Crœsus and Sir Pandarus—
    And the music played apace.
But of all that crowd I only saw
    A single, single face!

'Twas that of a girl whom I had known
    In the summers long ago,
When her breath was like the new-mown hay,
    Or the sweetest flowers that grow—
When her heart was light, and her soul was white
    As the winter's driven snow.

'Twas in our own New England
    She breathed the morning air;
'Twas the sunshine of New England
    That blended with her hair;
And modesty and purity
    Walked with her everywhere!

All day like a ray of light she played
   About old Harvey's mill;
And her grandsire held her on his knee
   In the evenings long and still,
And told her tales of Lexington,
   And the trench at Bunker's Hill—

And of the painted Wamponsags,
   The Indians who of yore
Builded their wigwams out of bark
   In the woods of Sagamore;
And how the godly Puritans
   Burnt witches by the score!

Or, touching on his sailor-life,
   He told how, years ago,
In the dark of a cruel winter night,
   In the rain and sleet and snow,
The good bark *Martha Jane* went down
   On the rocks off Holmes' Ho'!

The years flew by, and the maiden grew
　　Like a harebell in the glade;
The chestnut shadows crept in her eyes—
　　Sweet eyes that were not afraid
To look to heaven at morn or even,
　　Or any time she prayed!

She walked with him to the village church,
　　And his eyes would fill with pride
To see her walk with the man she loved—
　　To see them side by side!
Sweet Heaven! she were an angel now
　　If she had only died.

If she had only died!　Alas!
　　How keen must be the woe
That makes it better one should lie
　　Where the sunshine cannot go,
Than to live in this sunny world of ours.
　　Where the happy blossoms blow!

Would she had wed some country clown
   Before the luckless day
When her cousin came to that lowly home—
   Her cousin Richard May,
With his city airs and handsome eyes,
   To lead her soul astray!

One night they left the cottage—
   One night in the mist and rain;
And the old man never saw his child
   Nor Richard May again;
Never saw his pet in the clover patch,
   In the meadow, nor the lane.

Ah! never was a heart so torn
   Since this wild world began,
As day by day he looked for her,
   This pitiful old man.
"Where's my pretty maid?" he said,
   This pitiful old man.

Many a dreary winter came,
  And he had passed away;
And we never heard of her who fled
  In the night with Richard May;
Never knew if she were alive or dead
  Till I met her at the play!

And there she sat with her great brown eyes,
  They wore a troubled look;
And I read the history of her life
  As it were an open book;
And saw her Soul, like a slimy thing
  In the bottom of a brook.

There she sat in her rustling silk,
  With diamonds on her wrist,
And on her brow a slender thread
  Of pearl and amethyst.
" A cheat, a gilded grief!" I said,
  And my eyes were filled with mist.

I could not see the players play,
  I heard the music moan ;
It moaned like a dismal autumn wind,
  That dies in the woods alone ;
And when it stopped I heard it still,
  The mournful monotone !

What if the Count were true or false ?
  I did not care, not I ;
What if Camille for Armand died ?
  I did not see her die.
There sat a woman opposite
  Who held me with her eye !

The great green curtain fell on all,
  On laugh, and wine, and woe,
Just as death some day will fall
  'Twixt us and life, I know !
The play was done, the bitter play,
  And the people turned to go.

And did they see the Tragedy?
     They saw the painted scene;
They saw Armand, the jealous fool,
     And the sick Parisian quean;
But they did not see the Tragedy—
     The one I saw, I mean!

They did not see that cold-cut face,
     Those braids of golden hair;
Or, seeing her jewels, only said,
     "The lady's rich and fair."
But I tell you, 'twas the Play of Life,
     And that woman played Despair!

TWO LEAVES FROM A PLAY.

.

―――――

1.— *Hortense.*

O, BUT she loved him, and the death she died
Wrote Love across her bosom.   Fainter hearts
Had wept and pined themselves into the grave.
She was not fashioned of such gossamer;
For one bleak midnight, robed as for a fête,
With all her splendor, and her jewels on,
She sucked quick poison from a finger-ring,
And so they found her, in the morning—dead.
The pearls lay on her bosom like pale flowers
When no wind stirs them; with one waxen hand
She held his crumpled letter: in the room
Sat Silence and white Slumber!   So she died.

2.—*After the Masquerade.*

We've danced the night out, Madaline.

Pleasure is sick, and Music's self has grown

As languid as a weary ballet-girl!

There's not a dozen maskers in the hall.

How like the pictures on a wizard's glass

The particolored pageant has swept by—

Fools with their bells, and Monarchs with their
crowns,

Athenians, and bearded Mamalukes,

Death-heads and Satyrs, and weird shadows born

In the brains of crazy poets.   Yet so real—

Such bitter mimicry!   O, Madaline,

This is the very world in miniature:

We each wear dresses that become us not,

We each are maskers in a Carnival.

The spangles and the tinsel of our lives,

The soul in song, the jests above our wine,

Are pleasant lies that tell not what we are.

The Droll's at best a melancholy man;

His wit is only honey in a skull;

And though he glitter like a prism i' the light

His colors cannot hide the skeleton!

The Scholar is a cynic, and the Priest

A solemn epicurean in a cowl;

Philanthropy is politic: the Slave

Wears not such fetters as the Emperor.

And so, my love, Life plays at harlequin,

Smothers itself in ermine, or puts on

The icy front of virtue for effect.

A smile's a mask to hide a broken heart:

Fair words are masks, and all this blazoned world

Against the frozen opal in your ring,

There's no such mask as woman's tears may be!

KATHIE MORRIS.

AN IDYL.

————●————

1.

Au! fine it was that April time, when gentle
winds were blowing,
To hunt for pale arbutus-blooms that hide beneath the leaves,
To hear the slanting rain come down, and see
the clover growing,
And watch the airy swallows as they darted
round the eaves!

2.

You wonder why I dream to-night of clover that
    was growing
  So many years ago, my wife, when we were in
    our prime;
For, hark! the wind is in the flue, and Johnny
    says 'tis snowing,
  And through the storm the clanging bells ring
    in the Christmas time.

3.

I cannot tell, but something sweet about my
    heart is clinging.
  A vision and a memory—'tis little that I
    mind
The weary wintry weather, for I hear the robins
    singing,
  And the petals of the apple-blooms are ruffled
    in the wind!

4.

It was a sunny morn in May, and in the fragrant
    meadow
  I lay, and dreamed of one fair face, as fair and
        fresh as spring:
Would Kathie Morris love me? then in sunshine
    and in shadow
  I built up lofty castles on a golden wedding-
        ring!

5.

O, sweet it was to dream of her, the soldier's
    only daughter,
  The pretty pious Puritan, that flirted so with
        Will;
The music of her winsome mouth was like the
    laughing water
  That broke in silvery syllables by Farmer
        Philip's mill.

6.

And Will had gone away to sea; he did not leave
her grieving;
Her bonny heart was not for him, so reckless
and so vain;
And Will turned out a buccaneer, and hanged
was he for thieving
And scuttling helpless ships that sailed across
the Spanish Main.

7.

And I had come to grief for her, the scornful village beauty,
For, oh! she had a witty tongue could cut you
like a knife;
She scorned me with her haughty eyes, and I, in
bounden duty,
Did love her—loved her more for that, and
wearied of my life!

8.

And yet 'twas sweet to dream of her, to think
    her wavy tresses
  Might rest some happy, happy day, like sun-
    shine, on my cheek;
The idle winds that fanned my brow I dreamed
    were her caresses,
  And in the robin's twitterings I heard my
    sweetheart speak.

9.

And as I lay and thought of her, her fairy face
    adorning
  With lover's fancies, treasuring the slightest
    word she'd said,
'Twas Kathie broke upon me like a blushing
    summer morning,
  And a half-blown rosy clover reddened under-
    neath her tread!

10.

Then I looked up at Kathie, and her eyes were
full of laughter:
"O, Kathie, Kathie Morris, I am lying at
your feet;
Bend above me, say you love me, that you'll
love me ever after,
Or let me lie and die here, in the fragrant mea-
dow-sweet!"

11.

And then I turned my face away, and trembled
at my daring,
For wildly, wildly had I spoke, with flashing
cheek and eye;
And there was silence; I looked up, all pallid and
despairing,
For fear she'd take me at my word, and leave
me there to die.

12.

The silken fringes of her eyes upon her cheeks
    were drooping,
    Her merciless white fingers tore a blushing
      bud apart;
Then, quick as lightning, Kathie came, and kneel-
    ing half and stooping,
    She hid her bonny, bonny face against my
      beating heart.

13.

O, nestle, nestle, nestle there! the heart would
    give thee greeting;
    Lie thou there, all trustfully, in trouble and in
      pain;
This breast shall shield thee from the storm, and
    bear its bitter beating,
    These arms shall hold thee tenderly in sun-
      shine and in rain!

14.

Old sexton! set your chimes in tune, and let
there be no snarling,
Ring out a joyous wedding-hymn to all the
listening air;
And, girls, strew roses as she comes, the scornful, brown-eyed darling—
A princess, by the wavy gold and glistening
of her hair!

15.

Hark! hear the bells. The Christmas bells?
O, no; who set them ringing?
I think I hear our bridal-bells, and I with joy
am blind;
I smell the clover in the fields, I hear the robins
singing.
And the petals of the apple-blooms are ruffled
in the wind!

16.

Ah! Kathie, you've been true to me in fair and
    cloudy weather;
  Our Father has been good to us when we've
    been sorely tried:
I pray to God, when we must die, that we may
    die together,
  And slumber softly underneath the clover, side
    by side.

HASCHEESH.

1.

STRICKEN with thought, I staggered through the
      night;
The heavens leaned down to me with splendid
      fires;
The seven Pleiads, changed to magic lyres,
Made music as I went; and to my sight
A Palace shaped itself against the skies:
Great sapphire-studded portals suddenly
Opened upon vast Gothic galleries
Of gold and ebony, and I could see,
Through half-drawn curtains that let in the day,
Dim tropic gardens stretching far away!

2.

Ah! what a wonder seized upon my soul,
When from that structure of the upper airs
I saw unfold a flight of crystal stairs
For my ascending. . . . . Then I heard the roll
Of unseen oceans clashing at the Pole. . . .
A terror fell upon me . . . . a vague sense
Of near calamity.   O, lead me hence!
I shrieked, and lo! from out a darkling hole
That opened at my feet, crawled after me,
Up the broad staircase, creatures of huge size,
Fanged, warty monsters, with their lips and eyes
Hung with slim leeches sucking hungrily.——
Away, vile drug! I will avoid thy spell,
Honey of Paradise, black dew of Hell!

II.

HESPERIDES.

————◆————

If thy soul, Herrick, dwelt with me,
This is what my songs would be:

Hints of our sea-breezes, blent
With odors from the Orient;
Indian vessels deep with spice;
Star-showers from the Norland ice;
Wine-red jewels that seem to hold
Fire, but only burn with cold;
Antique goblets, strangely wrought, .
Filled with the wine of happy thought;

45

Bridal measures, dim regrets,
Laburnum buds and violets;
Hopeful as the break of day;
Clear as crystal; fresh as May;
Musical as brooks that run
O'er yellow shallows in the sun;
Soft as the glossy fringe that shades
The eyelids of thy fragrant maids;
Brief as thy lyrics, Herrick, are,
And polished as the bosom of a star!

THE CRESCENT AND THE CROSS.

KIND was my friend who, in the Eastern land,
Remembered me with such a gracious hand,
And sent this Moorish Crescent which has been
Worn on the tawny bosom of a queen.

No more it sinks and rises in unrest
To the soft music of her heathen breast;
No barbarous chief shall bow before it more,
No turban'd slave shall envy and adore!

I place beside this relic of the Sun
A Cross of Cedar brought from Lebanon,
Once borne, perchance, by some pale monk who
        trod
The desert to Jerusalem—and his God!

Here do they lie, two symbols of two creeds,
Each meaning something to our human needs,
Both stained with blood, and sacred made by faith,
By tears, and prayers, and martyrdom, and death.

That for the Moslem is, but this for me!
The waning Crescent lacks divinity:
It gives me dreams of battles, and the woes
Of women shut in hushed seraglios.

But when this Cross of simple wood I see,
The Star of Bethlehem shines again for me,
And glorious visions break upon my gloom—
The patient Christ, and Mary at the Tomb!

SONG.

1.

THE chestnuts shine through the cloven rind,
    And the woodland leaves are red, my dear;
The scarlet fuchsias burn in the wind—
    Funeral plumes for the Year!

2.

The Year which has brought me so much woe,
    That if it were not for you, my dear,
I should wish the fuchsias' fire might glow
    For me as well as the Year!

PISCATAQUA RIVER.

1860.

———◆———

Thou singest by the gleaming isles,
   By woods and fields of corn,
Thou singest, and the heaven smiles
   Upon my birthday morn.

But I within a city, I,
   So full of vague unrest,
Would almost give my life to lie
   An hour upon thy breast.

To let the wherry listless go,
  And, wrapped in dreamy joy,
Dip, and surge idly to and fro,
  Like the red harbor-buoy!

To sit in happy indolence,
  To rest upon the oars,
And catch the heavy earthy scents
  That blow from summer shores:

To see the rounded sun go down,
  And with its parting fires
Light up the windows of the town
  And burn the tapering spires!

And then to hear the muffled tolls
  From steeples slim and white,
And watch, among the Isles of Shoals,
  The Beacon's orange light.

O, River! flowing to the main
 Through woods and fields of corn,
Hear thou my longing and my pain
 This sunny birthday morn!

And take this song which sorrow shapes
 To music like thine own,
And sing it to the cliffs and capes
 And crags where I am known!

THE LUNCH.

A Gothic window, where a damask curtain
Made the blank daylight shadowy and uncertain:
A slab like agate on four eagle-talons
Held trimly up and neatly taught to balance:
A porcelain dish, o'er which in many a cluster
Plump grapes hung down, dead-ripe and without
     lustre:
A melon cut in thin delicious slices:
A cake that seemed mosaic-work in spices:
Two China cups with golden tulips sunny,
And rich inside with chocolate like honey;
And she and I the banquet-scene completing
With dreamy words—and very dainty eating!

HAUNTED.

A NOISOME mildewed vine
Crawls to the rotting eaves;
The gate has dropt from the rusty hinge
And the walks are strewn with leaves.

Close by the shattered fence
The red-clay road runs by
To a haunted wood, where the hemlocks groan
And the willows sob and sigh.

Among the dank lush flowers
The spiteful firefly glows,
And a woman steals by the stagnant pond
Wrapped in her burial-clothes.

There's a dark blue scar on her throat,
And ever she makes a moan;
And the humid lizards shine in the grass,
And the lichens weep on the stone,

And the Moon shrinks in a cloud,
And the traveller shakes with fear,
And an Owl on the skirts of the wood
Hoots, and says, Do you hear?

Go not there at night,
For a spell hangs over all—
The palsied elms, and the dismal road,
And the broken garden-wall.

O, go not there at night,

For a curse is on the place;

Go not there, for fear you meet

The Murdered face to face!

SONG.

1.

MERRY is the robin
   That pipes away his care,
And merry is the mackerel
   That leaps a yard in air!
And merry is the butter-cup
   Beneath the April sky,
And merry as the spring-time,
   Love, are you and I!

57

2.

Now the robin's chilly,
  And all his songs are done;
No more the spotted mackerel
  Leaps silvery in the sun.
O, mournful is the scarlet leaf,
  And mournful is the sky—
But merry as the spring-time,
  Love, are you and I!

MIRIAM'S WOE.

Miriam at the planter's door,
　　Her child upon her knee,
Sat as the twilight gathered round
　　The vale of Nacoochee.

Sat with an anguish in her eyes,
　　And forehead bended low—
Sat like a statue carved in stone,
　　All pallid with her woe!

59

By dark bayou and cypress-swamp,
  By rice-field and lagoon,
Her soul went wandering to the land
  That scorches in the noon!

And on the lover of her youth
  She turned her patient eyes,
And saw him sad, and faint, and sick
  Beneath those alien skies.

She saw him pick the cotton-blooms
  And cut the sugar-cane—
A ring of iron on his wrist,
  And round his heart a chain!

She saw him, when his work was done,
  Sit down in some lone place,
To dream of her, and weep for her,
  His hands across his face!

She heard the dear old violin
　That he was wont to play
At twilight, in their courting-time,
　When life was sweet as May!

Then suddenly a catbird called
　From out a neighboring tree,
And Miriam's soul came back again
　To the vale of Nacoochee.

And closer, closer to her heart
　She held the little child,
Who stretched its fragile hand to feel
　Her bosom's warmth, and smiled.

But she—she did not own a touch
　Of that fond little hand—
Great God! that such a thing should be
　Within a Christian land!

THE ROBIN.

From out the blossomed cherry-tops
Sing, blithsome Robin, chant and sing;
With chirp, and trill, and magic-stops
Win thou the listening ear of Spring!

For while thou lingerest in delight,
An idle poet, with thy rhyme,
The summer hours will take their flight
And leave thee in a barren clime.

62

Not all the autumn's brittle gold,
Nor sun, nor moon, nor star shall bring
The jocund spirit which of old
Made it an easy joy to sing!

So said a poet—having lost
The precious time when he was young—
Now wandering by the wintry coast
With empty heart and silent tongue.

IN THE OLD CHURCH-TOWER.

1859.

———

1.

In the old church-tower
   Hangs the bell;
And above it on the vane,
In the sunshine and the rain,
Cut in gold, Saint Peter stands,
With the keys in his two hands,
   And all is well!

64

2.

In the old church-tower
   Hangs the bell;
You can hear its great heart beat,
Ah! so loud, and wild, and sweet,
As the parson says a prayer
Over wedded lovers there,
   While all is well!

3.

In the old church-tower
   Hangs the bell,
Deep and solemn.   Hark! again,
Ah! what passion, and what pain!
With her hands upon her breast,
Some poor Soul has gone to rest
   Where all is well!

5

4.

In the old church-tower
  Hangs the bell—
An old friend that seems to know
All our joy and all our woe:
It is glad when we are wed,
It is sad when we are dead
  And all is well!

SONG.

———

Blow from the temples of the Sun,
　　Thou heavy-scented wind;
O, blow across the spicy isles
　　And strike the roses blind!

And kiss the eyes of my true-love,
　　And tell me if she be
Not lovelier than the Khaleef's wife
　　Beyond the Indian sea!

LAMIA.

"Go on your way, and let me pass.
    You stop a wild despair.
I would that I were turned to brass
    Like that grim dragon there,

"Which, couchant by the groined gate,
    In weather foul or fair,
Looks down serenely desolate,
    And nothing does but stare!

" What care I for the burgeoned year,
  The sad leaf or the gay?
Let Launcelot and Guinevere
  Their falcons fly this day.

" Twill be as royal sport, pardie,
  As falconers have tried
At Astolat—but let me be!
  I would that I had died.

" I met a woman in the glade:
  Her hair was soft and brown,
And long bent silken lashes weighed
  Her ivory eyelids down.

" I kissed her hand, I called her blest,
  I held her true and fair—
She turned to shadow on my breast,
  And melted in the air!

"And, lo! about me, fold on fold,
A golden serpent hung—
An eye of jet, a skin of gold,
A garnet for a tongue!

"O, let the petted falcons fly
Right merry in the sun;
But let me be! for I shall die
Before the year is done."

THE MAN AND THE HOUR.

As some rare jewel, sealed within a rock,
    Would ne'er have glittered in the sunny air,
Had not the lightning or an earthquake's shock
    Crumbled the ledge, and laid its splendor bare—
So do fine souls lie darkling in the earth
Until some mighty tumult heaves them forth.

Men of this land and lovers of these States!
    What master-spirit from the dark shall rise,
And, with a will inviolate as fate's,
    God-like and prudent, merciful and wise,
Do battle in God's name and set us right
Ere on our glory ruin broods and night!

December, 1860.

OUR COLORS AT FORT SUMTER.

1.

HERE's to the Hero of Moultrie,
The valiant and the true!
True to our Flag—by land and sea
Long may it wave for you!

2.

May never traitor's touch pollute
Those colors of the sky—
We want them pure, to wrap about
Our heroes when they die!

January, 1861.